Adapted by Alice Alfonsi

Based on the television series, "Lizzie McGuire", created by Terri Minsky

Part One is based on the episode written by Nancy Neufeld Callaway

Part Two is based on the episode written by Nina G. Bargiel & Jeremy J. Bargiel

Watch it on

New York

Printed in the United States of America

First Edition
1 3 5 7 9 10 8 6 4 2

Library of Congress Catalog Card Number: 2004113853

ISBN 0-7868-4702-6
For more Disney Press fun, visit www.disneybooks.com
Visit DisneyChannel.com

Lizzie McGuire

PART ONE

CHAPTER ONE

Why is my life so totally *lame*? Lizzie McGuire asked herself one Monday morning. Lately, nothing she did seemed seriously good or seriously bad. Just seriously boring.

As she trudged through the halls of Hillridge Junior High, Lizzie noticed some students gathering around a bulletin board. Her English teacher had just posted the grades from last Friday's big test.

Hey, she thought, quickening her pace

toward the group of kids, maybe this is the day I break out of my totally boring, average rut. Maybe this is the day I finally excel at something and make an A.

"Yes! I aced it again!" cried Ricky Mercado.

Of course he aced it, thought Lizzie. Ricky was reading Shakespeare back when I was still sounding out the vowels in *See Spot Run*.

Standing next to Ricky, Tanya Washington gave him a high five. "Look out, Harvard!" she squealed. Tanya, who had made an A also, was the regional spelling bee champ. Under pressure, Lizzie was lucky if she could spell *bee*.

After Ricky and Tanya strutted away, Lizzie moved closer to the bright orange roster her English teacher had posted. Students' names were listed alphabetically.

Lippin, Mattson, McGuire, Lizzie read silently to herself. Then her eyes moved to see the grade beside her name.

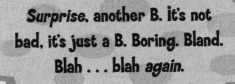

Surprise, another B. it's not bad, it's just a B. Boring. Bland. Blah . . . blah *again.*

Lizzie sighed and continued her walk down the hall. It was *not* a happy walk. Every ten feet she passed some amazingly accomplished classmate.

First there was Ivana Peters, bending and stretching by her locker. As a small child, Ivana had studied ballet in Moscow. Now she was performing professionally in her spare time, and everyone expected her two talented feet to take her to the top of the toe-dancing world.

After Ivana, Lizzie passed a group of science geeks. They were all gathered around Larry Tudgeman because he'd won yet another science fair prize over the weekend. His winning entry was some sort of way-complicated study of a molecule.

Ever notice that *everyone* seems to be great at something?

Even Tudgeman's science fair groupies were probably going to win Nobel prizes, thought Lizzie. And what am I destined to win in my totally average life span? The Blend-in Betty award. How lame is that?

Lizzie shook her head. This whole super-achiever thing was really starting to bug her. Just then, Lizzie spotted her two best friends, Miranda Sanchez and David "Gordo" Gordon.

Panic attack averted, she thought, striding

over to them. After all, being totally average and boring isn't so bad when your friends are right there beside you being totally average and boring with you!

Unfortunately, Lizzie quickly had to admit that her best friends were far from average and boring. For instance, Miranda was holding up a piece of chunky silver jewelry for Gordo to see.

"Hey, great necklace," Lizzie told Miranda. It was totally cool and unique.

"Thanks," said Miranda with a grin. "I made it out of a soda can."

Lizzie's brow furrowed.

See what I mean? All *I* can do with a soda can is recycle it.

"No, no," Gordo told Miranda, "don't turn that way—I'm losing my shot."

Lizzie grimaced when she noticed the digital camera in Gordo's hands. He was filming Miranda in another one of his "typical day at Hillridge" shoots.

Gordo's in search of his next documentary and I can barely take a Polaroid.

Miranda noticed Lizzie frowning. "What's up?" she asked.

"English test grades are up," Lizzie replied.

"Another B?" guessed Miranda.

"What else?" Lizzie said. "I'm so sick of getting Bs. I want an A at something."

"Hey, you could be an actress," Gordo

suggested brightly from behind his digital lens. "You look pretty good through the camera."

"You think?" asked Lizzie hopefully.

Gordo nodded supportively. "Sure."

"Cool," said Lizzie. She did a little spin in place, trying to make her hair whip around like Britney Spears.

Wow, thought Lizzie. Me. An actress—

Unfortunately, Lizzie failed to notice Gordo's backpack sitting on the floor two feet away. As she tripped over it and went flying, Gordo frowned. He removed the camera from his eye and blinked at Lizzie.

"Or a stuntwoman," he amended.

From the floor, Lizzie groaned, now totally convinced she would *never* be good at anything.

CHAPTER TWO

Monday didn't get much better. At the start of gym class, Coach Kelly announced that their physical education lesson would be taking place outside.

Great, thought Lizzie, as if wearing dorky gym clothes isn't embarrassing enough *inside*.

She and Miranda followed their teacher and the rest of the girls out to Hillridge's athletic field. Miranda nudged Lizzie and pointed to a couple of boys hanging out on the other side of the fence. They were laughing at the girls' baggy blue T-shirts and long, gray shorts, which were about as stylin' as prison uniforms.

Miranda rolled her eyes. "There is absolutely nothing happy about Mondays," she said, "especially with the dreaded and most-feared Coach Kelly."

"Yeah, Queen of the gym-nauseum," agreed Lizzie.

"Evil PE Sorceress," added Miranda.

Their teacher's nasty temper plus her obsession with deep knee bends and dodgeball had convinced Lizzie and Miranda they'd probably find a wicked-witch broomstick in her office closet. The woman just could not stop conjuring up new ways to totally humiliate them.

"I wonder what our new sport is this time," griped Miranda.

Lizzie sighed. "Whatever it is, I bet I'm just as bad at it as I was at archery."

Miranda winced. Both girls remembered the day Lizzie had pulled back her bow and let her arrow fly. Unfortunately, she'd missed the standing target by a mile. But it *had* hit something nearby—the left rear tire of their gym teacher's SUV.

"Coach Kelly shouldn't park her car so close to the field," Lizzie pointed out defensively. Really, she thought, is it my fault a steel-belted radial can't stand up to a puny, little arrow tip?

"Rhythmic gymnastics!" announced Coach Kelly.

Lizzie and Miranda jumped slightly at the booming sound of the big woman's voice. Coach Kelly had opened up a box filled with rhythmic gymnastics equipment: ribbons, hoops, balls, and clubs.

The big teacher grabbed a white hoop, hung it around her thick neck, and gave it a spin. Then she began to twist and jiggle to make the hoop continue its circular motion.

Miranda and Lizzie rolled their eyes at the ridiculous sight of Coach Kelly's throat doing the hula hoop. *This* is a *sport*? Lizzie thought.

"A combination of gymnastics and ballet, requiring supreme skill and coordination," Coach Kelly explained.

And floppy shoes and a red clown nose.

"Originating hundreds of years ago, it

became an official Olympic sport in 1984," the teacher continued.

Lizzie turned to Miranda. "You've got to be kidding me," she whispered.

Miranda shook her head. "This is a pimple on the face of women's sports."

"Yeah," agreed Lizzie. "You think she gets paid *extra* for humiliating us?" It happened so often that it was the only logical explanation.

"You can use the ball, the hoop, the clubs, or the ribbon, in any combination, but let's just start with the basics for today," said the coach.

"Girls' PE totally sucks," Miranda whispered to Lizzie.

"Yeah," Lizzie agreed quietly, "they don't make the boys do freaky stuff like this. They get to do all the cool things."

"Any volunteers?" Coach Kelly bellowed.

"No," Miranda blurted out.

Lizzie's eyes widened as Coach Kelly slowly turned in their direction. Miranda instantly looked horrified. She hadn't meant to say that so loudly!

"Inside voice, inside voice," Miranda squeaked to Lizzie in total panic.

"Miranda!" cried the teacher. "Did I just hear you *volunteer* to demonstrate?"

Miranda knew it wasn't a question. "Uh . . ." she said.

"Good," snapped the coach. "Why don't you show us how it's done?"

Miranda tentatively stepped forward. The coach held out two clubs—the kind Lizzie usually saw jugglers throwing in a circus. Miranda took the clubs. After a nervous breath, she tried twirling them, but they got away from her and went flying over the field. With a terrible crash, they landed in the aluminum bleachers.

"Oops," said Miranda sheepishly. "I'm gonna go get those . . . bye!"

As Lizzie's best friend hustled across the grass to retrieve the clubs, Kate Sanders and her posse of cheerleaders quietly began to snicker.

Lizzie narrowed her eyes at Kate, but she just sneered back. Then she formed an *L* with her thumb and index finger and put it up to her forehead. *Loser*, she mouthed to Lizzie.

As Coach Kelly spun around, Kate instantly dropped her hand and gave the teacher one of her sickeningly sweet, straight-A student smiles.

Coach Kelly's expression brightened. "Kate," she said with admiration. "Why don't *you* show us how it's *really* done."

Lizzie rolled her eyes. Coach Kelly just loved Kate—which was no big surprise. The girl was not only head cheerleader, she was supergood at just about everything they did in gym class.

With a toss of her hair, Kate walked up to the coach, who handed her another set of clubs. "Okay," said Kate with totally fake humility, "let's see if I can . . ."

After throwing Lizzie one last "I'm all that, and you're not" sneer, Kate began to twirl the clubs. For a few seconds, she actually looked like she knew what she was doing, but then it came time to toss them, and both heavy clubs came crashing down on top of Kate's right foot.

"Ow, ow, ow!" cried Kate, shocked and humiliated.

Everyone began to laugh. Kate whipped around, instantly silencing her crew of cheerleaders with a killer look.

"Looks like you'll need a little extra practice, Kate," Coach Kelly advised.

"There must be some mistake," Kate protested. "I'm good at everything. Can I just try again?"

The teacher was about to answer when she noticed one student was still laughing—Lizzie McGuire.

Miranda had returned from the bleachers by now and nudged her best friend to settle down already. But Lizzie couldn't help herself. Kate was the Queen of Mean, the first person to make fun of any kid who messed up anything, even a little. Lizzie doubled over, unable to stop her giggles at the sight of seeing Princess Perfect finally get what was coming to her.

Unfortunately, Lizzie's teacher didn't see it that way. "Lizzie McGuire?" snapped the coach. "Something amusing you?"

"No, no, not really," said Lizzie, finally composing herself.

"Then amuse me with your ribbon skills," the coach barked.

Ribbon *skills?* Lizzie thought, eyeing the long white ribbon attached to the short stick. The coach was holding it out to her, waiting for Lizzie to take it.

"Okay, um . . . Coach," said Lizzie, hoping to talk her way out of this. "I—I don't think I really know how to—"

"Flunk?" barked the coach. "You need some help?"

Lizzie gulped. "No." She didn't want to embarrass herself. But she didn't want to flunk, either, so she reluctantly stepped forward and held out her hand. Coach Kelly placed the stick against her palm and Lizzie's fingers closed around it. That's when it happened. Lightning struck—the closest thing to magic Lizzie had ever felt.

The stick and the ribbon suddenly made

absolute sense to her. She began to swirl the stick in wide arcs and the ribbon trailed behind it, flowing beautifully through the air like a stream of floating white water.

In Lizzie's head, she could hear the dance beat to one of her favorite Britney songs, and she began to move the ribbon to it, swirling it first in rhythmic circles, then in rippling waves.

Finally, Lizzie spun like Britney, but this time there was no backpack to trip her up, and the ribbon swirled around her in a perfect spiral of weightless white.

The entire class stood watching Lizzie with wide eyes—except Kate, who glared at her rival through a haze of rage. But, at the moment, no one cared about Kate. All eyes were on Lizzie. She was poetry in motion. Miranda's jaw dropped in amazement, and everyone, even Coach Kelly, appeared impressed by Lizzie's natural talent.

Finally Lizzie finished. With a smile she handed the ribbon's stick back to the stunned gym teacher.

Well, that's just perfect. I find the thing I'm great at—and it's the stupidest thing in the world. What's next? River dancing?

CHAPTER THREE

After class, Lizzie and Miranda went back to the locker room to change out of their gym clothes. They were almost finished when they noticed Kate hopping alongside Coach Kelly, who had just finished wrapping Kate's injured foot in an elastic bandage.

"Hey, Coach," said Kate between desperate hops. "Um, I figured out why I dropped the clubs on my foot. You see, I still had moisturizer on my hands to keep my skin soft and supple. Can you believe it? Anyway, I was just hoping I could have a second chance, if that would at all be possible."

Kate threw the coach a tense smile. The teacher thought it over a moment. "Okay, Kate," she finally said and handed her the ribbon.

Kate's jaw dropped. "Now?"

"Yeah."

By this time, the entire locker room of girls had noticed Kate begging for a second chance. A hush fell over the lockers. All eyes were on Kate.

Kate swallowed nervously as she noticed the audience. "It'd be my pleasure," she told Coach Kelly with forced cheerfulness. Then she turned around and noticed Lizzie staring at her. Kate's sickeningly sweet expression instantly turned sour.

"I don't care if this is dorky," she rasped just

loud enough for Lizzie to hear. "It's just one more thing that I'm better at than you are. Watch and learn."

Kate began to twirl the ribbon. But she just couldn't duplicate Lizzie's effortless performance on the athletic field, and the ribbon ended up wrapping around her legs. The harder Kate tried, the tighter the tangle became.

The gym teacher sighed. "Okay, then. Are we finished now?"

"No, wait!" Kate cried. Her ankles were now practically mummified by the rhythmic-gymnastics ribbon, but she still couldn't accept defeat. "There's something . . . wrong . . . with this . . . stupid . . . ribbon!" she cried, flailing around with the stick and what was left of the white ribbon.

"Thank you, Kate," said Coach Kelly, in a tone that said, *Just let it go already.* Lizzie almost laughed out loud. Then she heard Coach Kelly add, "May I have a moment alone with Lizzie?"

What?! thought Lizzie in a panic. Why does Coach Army Drill Sergeant Kelly want a moment alone with me? Then Lizzie remembered Miranda standing beside her and sighed with relief.

Thank goodness my best friend would never leave me alone with Coach Kelly.

Lizzie turned to grab Miranda's arm, but the girl was already outie!

Uh, maybe it's time for that "best friend" talk.

With nowhere to run, Lizzie suddenly found herself facing the dreaded gym teacher—a woman whose angry bellows could probably be heard in space. The teacher gestured for Lizzie to sit down on a locker room bench.

"Lizzie," Coach Kelly began, sitting down beside her, "in all my years of teaching, I've never seen someone take to rhythmic gymnastics like you. You're like a duck to water. Like a bird to the sky. You're like a—"

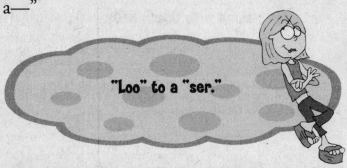

"Loo" to a "ser."

Lizzie shrugged. "Well, I guess I *was* pretty good," she admitted.

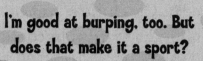

I'm good at burping, too. But does that make it a sport?

"Lizzie," the coach continued, "I want you to represent our school in the upcoming Rhythmic Gymnastics Regional Competition."

Lizzie blinked in shock. There had to be some mistake. She was Blend-in Betty, Average Annie. Nobody ever singled her out for anything special, least of all to represent the school in a competition—even if it was as seriously lame as rhythmic gymnastics.

"Excuse me?" Lizzie mumbled, thinking she'd probably misunderstood the teacher.

But she hadn't. Coach Kelly patted her on the back and assured her, "You're an incredibly talented athlete."

"Really?" asked Lizzie, still in shock.

"No," the coach had to admit. The truth was, until today, Coach Kelly had considered Lizzie McGuire a fairly uncoordinated, unmotivated, borderline spastic PE student. "But you are good at this," she declared.

That was almost a compliment.

Lizzie bit her lip in confusion. She knew it was flattering for the coach to offer her this chance, but the truth was, she didn't feel all that happy about it. "Maybe I should think about this," she told the teacher.

"Think about it," said the coach with a nod. "We'll talk later."

Meanwhile, outside the locker-room doors, Miranda and Gordo were hanging in the hall.

At the moment, Gordo wasn't too happy. He'd been filming kids all day, but a perfect subject for his documentary had yet to show itself.

A few steps away, Kate and her cheerleading crew were dishing dirt. Miranda didn't like the way they were glancing in her direction and laughing. She tried to ignore them, but when they mentioned Lizzie's name and laughed again, Miranda called out, "Something *funny*?"

"Yeah," snapped Kate. "Your friend. Tell her she must be really proud to have finally found her calling. Queen of the Ribbon Dorks."

What a witch, thought Miranda. She coolly narrowed her eyes at the cheer beast. "Face it, Kate," she replied. "You're just mad because Lizzie's *great* at it and you *stink* at it."

Kate glared at Miranda but didn't say

another word. She simply spun on her good heel and limped away.

I guess Kate can't argue with the truth, thought Miranda, watching Kate's pom-pom posse trail behind her. "See ya," cried Miranda. "Wouldn't want to be ya!"

Just then, Lizzie came out of the locker room and crossed over to her friends.

"So what did Coach Kelly want?" Gordo asked. He'd just filmed the whole nasty exchange between Miranda and Kate and was considering a documentary titled *Survivor: Junior High*. Now he turned his lens on Lizzie.

"Well . . ." Lizzie began, and inside of two minutes, she'd brought Gordo and Miranda up to date with her life thus far, including the coach's offer to have her represent Hillridge at the Rhythmic Gymnastics Regional Competition.

"But, I shouldn't do it, right?" finished Lizzie. "I mean, we think it's ridiculous, don't we?"

Lizzie waited for Miranda to agree, but Lizzie's best friend didn't answer right away. Miranda was too busy thinking how cool it would be for Lizzie to show up Kate by winning a gold medal in something at which Kate totally stunk.

"Don't we?" Lizzie prompted. "Think it's ridiculous?"

"No," Miranda finally replied, "it's cool."

"Oh, come on, Miranda," said Lizzie. "We both know rhythmic gymnastics is lame."

"*Lame* is such a strong word," said Miranda. "It's . . . lame-*ish*."

Gordo just grinned. "But the important thing is I finally have a topic for my documentary: *The Making of a Champion*."

"And it's something you're better at than Kate," Miranda pointed out.

Lizzie thought it over. "True. I do like that part."

"So you are gonna do it, right?" coaxed Gordo.

Lizzie sighed. Coach Kelly wanted her to do it. Miranda and Gordo wanted her to do it. But for some reason, Lizzie herself just wasn't sure.

"I don't know," she finally said.

CHAPTER FOUR

"So you think I should do it?" Lizzie asked.

"An Olympic sport! Absolutely!" cried Lizzie's mother.

As the McGuire family sat down to dinner that evening, Lizzie broke her big news about Coach Kelly wanting her to enter the Rhythmic Gymnastics Regional Competition. Her parents were ecstatic, of course. What else would they be? Lizzie thought. The "Parental Handbook" told them they were supposed to go gaga over stuff like this.

"Maybe next time they'll have the Olympics someplace really good," said Lizzie's father as he reached for a platter of corn on the cob. "Like Hawaii . . . or Orlando."

"You guys don't think rhythmic gymnastics is just a little . . . *lame?*" Lizzie asked.

"Ding-ding-ding!" cried her little brother, Matt. "We have a winner!"

Mr. McGuire frowned. "Matthew."

Lizzie threw up her hands. "See," she said, "even a lame-o knows it's lame."

"Thank you," Matt began to say—until he realized he'd just been insulted. "Hey, wait a minute!"

"Then again," added Lizzie, ignoring him, "how many talents do you get in one lifetime?"

"I have six," Matt declared. "One is that curlicue thing I do with my tongue. Two is saying anyone's name backward: Tarzan . . . Nazrat. Three is eating spoonfuls of wasabi. Four is I always win staring contests with dogs—"

Lizzie rolled her eyes at jerk-face's idiotic prattle. Ignoring him, she turned to her dad. "Plus, you've always said I could do anything if I set my mind to it."

Matt's eyes widened at that. "Really?" he asked then narrowed his gaze on his father. "You never told *me* that."

Mr. McGuire frowned again. "You sure?"

As Matt scratched his spiky-haired head, Lizzie sighed. Whatever her dad did or did not tell Matt, she knew one thing: anything the evil little porcupine's devious mind got set on doing would probably require alerting the Department of Homeland Security.

After dinner, Lizzie went to her room and brooded for hours about rhythmic gymnastics. On the one hand, she thought the sport was stupid. But on the other hand, her parents, friends, and teacher all thought she should compete in it.

Lizzie didn't really like the sport, but was that a good enough reason to bail and let everybody in her life down?

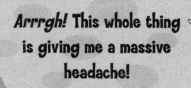

Arrrgh! This whole thing is giving me a massive headache!

Finally, it was time for bed, and Lizzie crawled under the covers. She lay awake, tossing and turning, until dreamland took over. . . .

"And the gold medal goes to . . . Lizzie McGuire!"

Lizzie saw herself standing at the highest podium in a vast European stadium. Tens of thousands of spectators rose to their feet and applauded. An official in a blue blazer came over and hung a big, shiny medal around her neck.

Suddenly, the dream shifted, and Lizzie found herself riding in an open convertible. Her car was leading a parade of marching bands and elaborate floats. Over the crowded boulevard hung a huge banner that read, WELCOME HOME, LIZZIE! HILLRIDGE IS PROUD OF YOU! As the crowd chanted her name, she waved and showed everyone her gold medal.

The scene shifted again, and Lizzie saw herself coming down to breakfast to find her family eating cereal. The box on the table read: "Toasted Oats, the cereal of rhythmic gymnastics gold-medal winners." Her picture was on the box.

In her sleep, Lizzie rolled over—and smiled.

The next day at school, Gordo caught up with Miranda to talk over the Lizzie situation. As the two of them flopped down on the quad's grass, Gordo declared, "We can't push Lizzie into doing something shameful just because I want to make a documentary and you want to one-up Kate."

"We can't?" asked Miranda.

Gordo frowned.

"Okay," Miranda quickly amended, "we can't. You're right."

"Being humiliated during puberty can have deep and lasting psychological consequences," he explained.

Miranda sighed. "You've been into your dad's shrink files again, haven't you?"

Gordo shrugged. "His Tuesday at 3:30 is really scary."

Just then, Lizzie strode up to them. Her confidence level was through the roof, and she was practically bouncing on her heels.

"Lizzie, we need to talk to you," said Miranda in a superserious voice.

"Oh, good!" Lizzie cried excitedly. "I've been up thinking about rhythmic gymnastics all night and I've had a big attitude adjustment."

"And how do you *feel* about that?" asked Gordo, channeling his psychiatrist father.

"Great," said Lizzie with supreme confidence. "I can win this thing, I know I can. I feel strong and determined. And I wanted to find something I was good at, so I've found it. And I'm one hundred percent going for the gold."

"You are?" asked Miranda in total confusion. Less than twenty-four hours before, her best friend had been tearing herself up over not wanting to compete. Now she sounded like one of those maniacs on the sports-drink commercials.

"Well, I think we've had a breakthrough," offered Gordo.

"Thanks," said Lizzie. Then she bounded off again, on her way to her next class.

"What do we do now?" Miranda asked Gordo, still perplexed. She'd been ready to support Lizzie's decision to dump the gymnastics thing. This "going for the gold" stuff was really throwing her—not to mention the fact that Lizzie didn't even *sound* like Lizzie anymore.

Gordo just shrugged. He wasn't about to question a decision that made his life easier. What came next was easy as far as he was concerned—

"Lights, camera, action!"

CHAPTER FIVE

Buzz! Buzz! Buzz!

With her eyes still closed, Lizzie smacked the OFF button on her alarm clock the next morning. Why does dawn have to come so *early?* she wailed to herself.

It was five A.M., time to rise and shine. In one hour, two things would happen—the sun would come up (let's hope) and Coach Kelly would be meeting her on the athletic field so she could get in a practice session before school started. She'd have to attend a practice session *after* school, too. That was the schedule Lizzie had agreed to when she'd accepted the teacher's invitation to compete in the rhythmic gymnastic regionals in three weeks.

But Lizzie wasn't used to getting up so early, and she immediately fell back to sleep—until someone nearly yanked her arm out of its socket! Opening her eyes, Lizzie saw Gordo standing next to her bed, shaking her awake. He was already filming her for his *Making of a Champion* documentary.

Arrrgh, Gordo! Lizzie thought. How about renaming your movie *Making Yourself Scarce* and letting me sleep?

But it was too late. She'd already agreed to let him sleep over last night in Matt's room just so he could film her very first moments of training. Obviously, he'd heard her alarm. Now he was ready to be Mr. Director, and she was ready to scream. Throwing off her covers, she stumbled out of bed.

In the McGuire kitchen, Gordo filmed Lizzie's mother cracking six eggs into a water glass. According to Coach Kelly, this raw egg breakfast was the protein drink of champions. According to Lizzie, however, the disgusting goop was undrinkable. With a quick change of plan, Lizzie dumped the eggs into a frying pan and ate them scrambled.

I have my limits, she decided. And Rocky I'm not.

Dressed in a T-shirt and sweatpants, Lizzie met up with her teacher at school and began her workout.

Every day it was the same: she jogged the field, and practiced with the hoop, the ribbon, and the clubs.

To build strength, Lizzie did a zillion sit-ups and lifted weights. To increase flexibility, she did stretch after stretch and split after split—with Coach Kelly pushing her harder and harder at every practice.

Rhythmic gymnastics became Lizzie's entire life—two practices every day during the school week and all-day practices on Saturdays and Sundays. She spent every waking moment thinking about her routine. She walked through her house spinning her rhythmic gymnastics hoop, brushed her teeth twirling her rhythmic gymnastics ribbon. And every night, she dreamed of little rhythmic gymnastic clubs with smiley faces doing dance routines.

Two weeks into her killer practice schedule, Lizzie was exhausted.

"Whoa," said Miranda, seeing her best friend leaning, half-asleep against her locker one morning. "You look like Neve Campbell at the end of *Scream*."

"Which is pretty good compared to how I feel," said Lizzie through a yawn. "I'm hurt. I'm tired. I'm hungry. And I wish they would vote me off the island."

"'Morning, superstar!" said Gordo brightly. He walked up to Lizzie, looking through his digital camera lens—as usual. "Did I mention that you look awesome on film? This *Making of a Champion* documentary is turning out so cool. You better get an Oscar speech ready."

Just then, Kate and her posse strolled by— of course, it was her posse doing the "strolling." Kate's foot was still bandaged, so her "stroll" was more of a pathetic limp-hop.

"Well," Kate sneered at Lizzie, "if it isn't Miss Rhythmic Gymnastics."

Well, if it isn't Miss Clubfoot.

"What's your e-mail, Lizzie? Lizzie at big-giant-loser dot com?"

Gordo lifted his digital camera higher. "Could you say that one more time for the camera, Kate?" he asked. "I'm trying to cast the part of the bitter, *talentless* girl."

Kate glared at him.

Lizzie sighed. She didn't see any reason they should still be fighting about this. "Kate, you're great at everything," she said sincerely. "Why can't you let someone be better than you at one thing?"

Kate lifted her chin. "Because I'm not about to sit back and let the dorks take over. You better watch your step, McGuire."

Lizzie narrowed her eyes. "I'm not the one with the ankle brace."

Kate sputtered, but she couldn't think of a good comeback. So, with an angry huff, she simply turned and limp-hopped away.

* * *

After school that day, Lizzie worked harder than ever on her routine. It was an amazing practice session, and Gordo caught it on film.

Lizzie threw the hoop high into the air, performed two perfect cartwheels, and caught the hoop as she finished in a perfect arch and an amazing split. It was a thing of beauty.

"Excellent!" cried Coach Kelly. "Again. Give me five more of those. And really make 'em sing."

Lizzie nodded and walked back to her starting position. As she did, Gordo stopped filming to check his camera. Then something caught his eye across the field and he slowly brought his camera back up. With the press of a button, he zoomed in to get a close-up shot.

Watching all alone on the other side of the fence was Kate Sanders. She was green with envy.

From Kate's point of view, she'd seen enough. She left the field and walked straight back into the school building. On the second floor, Kate peeked through a door and found exactly the person she was looking for—Larry Tudgeman. He was working alone in the science lab on an extra-credit project.

Of course, thought Kate, what *else* would a social zero be doing after school? Carefully, she glanced up and down the empty hall. She had to make absolutely sure no one saw her talking to the likes of Larry *Dork*man. When she was satisfied the coast was clear, she walked into the science lab.

"Hi, Larry," she said, her voice dripping with fake sweetness.

Tudgeman tried not to look stunned. "Hi, K-K-Kate."

"You know my name?" she cried with mock surprise. "I didn't even think you noticed me."

"Me?" asked Larry in total shock. "Not notice you?" A nervous laugh erupted from him. It sounded like a donkey braying. Kate tried hard not to show her total disgust. Instead, she turned her attention to his petri dishes.

"Wow. That looks *so* complicated!" she gushed.

Larry shrugged. "Not really. I'm just growing some penicillin-resistant strains of bacteria."

Kate stepped back in horror. "Oh."

"No, just kidding." Larry grinned. "It's mold."

"Of course it is," said Kate, smiling sweetly while secretly wanting to smack the stupid geek grin off his dork face. Who joked about bacteria, for cripes sake!

Swallowing her revulsion, Kate moved closer. "Larry, could I ask you a little *favor*?"

With puppy dog eyes, Larry looked up. The prettiest, most popular girl in school had come to him for a favor. How could he refuse?

The days sped by, and soon it was the night before the big regional rhythmic gymnastics meet. Mrs. McGuire popped her head inside Lizzie's bedroom to show her the final adjustments she'd made to her costume. But Lizzie wasn't there.

Mrs. McGuire checked the family room next, then the back porch swing, but Lizzie wasn't in any of her usual places. She finally found Lizzie in the kitchen.

"Honey, you want to try this on?" Mrs. McGuire asked, holding up Lizzie's costume. Suddenly, she stopped and sniffed the air. "Oh, that smells good. What are you making?"

"Chocolate chip cookies," said Lizzie flatly.

Mrs. McGuire frowned. "Is something bothering you?" she asked.

"No, why?" said Lizzie.

"Well," replied her mother, "the night before you started Middle School, you made brownies. When your parakeet flew away, you made muffins. When Miranda went to summer camp, you made banana bread. You're *baking.* Something must be bothering you."

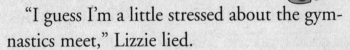

What's bothering me is I'm trying to win a gold medal in geek.

"I guess I'm a little stressed about the gymnastics meet," Lizzie lied.

"Oh, honey, you're working so hard, and you're so good at it," said her mother.

Lizzie shrugged. Sorry, Mom, she thought, but you're quoting page 103 in the *Mother-Daughter Handbook*. Sounds good on paper, but in the real world it's not gonna help.

"You know what?" her mother continued. "The most important thing is that you're doing something you love, and you're giving it your best shot. And your dad and I, we're going to be proud of you no matter what."

Lizzie nodded. More of same, she thought, as her mother dunked a finger in the mixing bowl and tasted the cookie dough.

"But I have a feeling you're going to win," said Mrs. McGuire with a grin.

Her grin was so genuine, Lizzie actually started to feel better—until Matt burst in.

"Of course she is," he blurted out, grabbing a cookie off the cooling rack then shoving it into his mouth. "She's the dork champion of the world!"

CHAPTER SIX

"That was Tracy Curtis, from Fair Oaks Middle School. Next up, Lizzie McGuire from Hillridge Junior High!"

When the announcer introduced Lizzie at the regionals the next day, she felt a fluttering in her stomach. All her practicing, all her hard work, had come down to this single performance.

Everyone was here. Her parents, her coach, her friends—even her enemies. Kate Sanders had shown up with her catty clique, and Lizzie knew she wasn't here to cheer. The Queen of Mean was dying to see Lizzie royally mess up.

With a deep breath, Lizzie shook her head clear of all her thoughts—good and bad—and took her place in the center of the big blue mat. *Okay,* she thought, *let's get this over with already*!

Underneath the colorful banners on the walls, hundreds of people filled the gymnasium bleachers. All eyes were on her, including her mother and father, who were obviously nervous wrecks through their smiles and waves.

On the sidelines stood Gordo, his digital camera whirring away. Trying to get the perfect angle, he moved along the edge of the mat and tripped over an equipment bag. Catching himself, he happened to look up—

and what he saw among the shadowy rafters above made him very suspicious. Using the camera's zoom lens, he took a closer look, then motioned for Miranda to come over.

"Gordo, what are you looking at?" she asked.

He told her what he suspected and she quickly left the gymnasium. Just then, the music started, echoing through the vast room, and Lizzie began her hoop routine with a series of spins and poses. After a graceful triple turn, a beautiful split-leap, and three flawless cart-wheels, the crowd applauded, and Lizzie grinned.

Gordo filmed it all with care. Then, halfway through her routine, Lizzie finished three aerial vaults and tossed the hoop high into the air. On the mat, she somersaulted, then reached up to catch the hoop she'd thrown—

But the hoop never came down! Not sure what to do, Lizzie waited for the hoop for one second, two, three . . .

Note to self:
Bring extra hoop.

"Lizzie!" Gordo called softly from the sidelines. When she looked over, he tossed her a ribbon.

By the next beat of music, Lizzie was continuing her routine—smoothly substituting ribbon tricks in place of the missing hoop.

On the sidelines, Gordo instantly knew what had gone wrong. Before Lizzie's routine began, he'd spotted Larry Tudgeman in the rafters. Clearly, Tudgeman had snagged the hoop to embarrass Lizzie—and Gordo could easily guess why. With a quick zoom of his camera, he focused on Kate Sanders in the audience. Just as he suspected, she looked pleased as punch with Lizzie's missing hoop.

By now, Miranda was on the catwalk that surrounded the gym's rafters. "Drop it, Tudgeman," she growled when she reached him.

Larry spun around in surprise. Lizzie's hoop was in his hand. "But I can't," he pleaded. "Kate won't love me anymore."

Miranda narrowed her eyes and lifted the fire extinguisher she'd picked up in the hallway downstairs. "Maybe this is empty," she told him, then pointed it at his head. "Do you feel lucky, Tudgeman? Huh? Do ya?"

Larry's eyes widened and he dropped the hoop. On the floor below, the hoop came sailing back down just as Lizzie was finishing her routine. She'd been completing a graceful arch when she caught sight of it falling—by now, catching it was automatic, and she snagged it with ease, finishing her routine with a magnificent split.

The audience went wild! From their point of view the disappearing and reappearing hoop was an ingenious part of Lizzie's performance. The judges agreed. Her scores were the highest of the day.

Kate was furious when she heard the applause. And the brilliant scores made her see red. I'm going to strangle Larry with my bare hands, she vowed to herself, jumping up from her bleacher seat. But after she slammed through the gymnasium's door, she found her pathway blocked.

Gordo had stepped right out in front of her, his camera rolling. "Going somewhere, Kate?" he asked, zooming in for a reaction shot.

Kate quickly masked her furious expression. "Just . . . getting . . . a little air."

"Tell it to the camera, sunshine," quipped Gordo as Miranda appeared with Larry Tudgeman at fire extinguisher point.

Gordo and Miranda exchanged a quick smile. Thanks to a little best friend teamwork, Kate and Larry were totally busted!

The awards ceremony took place at the end of the day, and Lizzie was stunned by the results.

"First place goes to Lizzie McGuire!" cried the announcer, and the crowd cheered. It was just like her dream. One of the judges placed a gold medal around her neck, and tons of people came over to congratulate her.

"We are so proud of you," gushed Mrs. McGuire, rushing up to Lizzie.

"Our little champion," said Mr. McGuire

as he gave her a big hug. "You were great sweetie, really. Look at your medal!"

"That's just great," said Lizzie. She cleared her throat, "but can I be honest with you?"

"Always," said Mrs. McGuire.

"Well," Lizzie began, "I totally appreciate how supportive you've been—"

"Lizzie, you don't have to thank us," her mother interrupted.

"We've loved every minute of it, honey—" added her father.

"I wasn't finished," said Lizzie flatly.

"Oh," said her parents.

They looked a little hurt and she felt bad. "No, really, you guys have been awesome," she said quickly. "But that time when the hoop was missing was the happiest time of my life."

Mr. and Mrs. McGuire looked at each other in confusion. "I don't understand," said Lizzie's mom.

"Yeah," agreed her dad.

Lizzie sighed. Then finally came clean with how she honestly felt. "I hate rhythmic gymnastics."

Mrs. McGuire still looked confused. "Oh, but you're so great at it."

"Yeah," said Mr. McGuire again.

"Well, that's just about the only part I *do* like," she admitted. "But if I don't even like it, why waste my time doing it?"

Her parents shared a look of concern. Lizzie knew they didn't want to raise a quitter—but that was one of the reasons she went through with the competition. She didn't want to let everybody down. Now that it was over, she had to stand up for herself. Otherwise, she'd be forced to spend almost every waking hour of her life pursuing somebody else's goal, somebody else's dream.

"I'd rather work extra hard at something I

do love, even if it takes a little longer," Lizzie told them. "Is that okay?"

"Of course it's okay," said her father.

Her mother nodded. "Honey, whatever you decide to do, your dad and I are going to be there cheering for you."

Lizzie smiled with extreme relief. "Even if it's dogsledding across Alaska?"

Mr. McGuire scratched his chin. "You know, I think *that* we'd have to watch on the big-screen TV."

By the early evening, Lizzie, Miranda, and Gordo were hanging in Lizzie's bedroom, eating popcorn and playing cards. Lizzie was incredibly happy. For the first time in weeks she actually had time to be with her friends. And tomorrow morning she would finally be able to sleep past the crack of dawn!

Plus, now that the competition was finally

over, she had to admit she was also pretty jazzed about winning that gold medal.

"You guys really saved my butt," she told her best friends.

"We did," said Gordo. "We know."

"You'll pay us back somehow," said Miranda.

Pay them back? thought Lizzie. "Hey," she protested, "what ever happened to, 'that's what friends are for'?"

"Please," said Miranda with a wave of her hand, "that's *so* last millennium."

Lizzie laughed. "So, Gordo, do we finally get to see your masterpiece?"

"Actually, it turned out a little differently than I'd planned," Gordo admitted. He pulled out his digital camera and ran the movie. The three friends watched on the camera's small view screen.

Making of a Champion didn't just include

shots of Lizzie training hard and winning the regionals. It featured shots of Kate acting totally green with envy from start to finish.

"Do you realize what this means?" said Miranda.

"Yeah," said Lizzie with a grin, "solid proof that Kate Sanders is actually jealous of *me*!"

The next week at school, Lizzie walked down the same old hallways she always did at Hillridge, but things just didn't look the same to her anymore. Since she'd won her gold medal, all those outstanding students she passed every day . . . well, they just didn't seem quite so superior.

Take Ricky Mercado, thought Lizzie as she passed by him checking out his excellent grades on the bulletin board. Straight-A student. Studies 24/7 . . .

Smart, but destined to
be lonely and dateless.

Then there was Ivana Peters, ballerina
supreme, doing her usual stretches by her
locker . . .

Too skinny. And
destined for a double
bunion-ectomy.

Finally, there was Larry Tudgeman and his
geeky science fair friends, in a huddle over yet
another amazing project . . .

Destined to be . . . gazillionaires!
Call me!

In the end, Lizzie realized none of her class-mates had actually changed. *She* had. With some really hard work and the backing of her two best friends, she'd finally excelled at something. Okay, so that something was lamer than river dancing, but it proved she could actually go for the gold and get it—and that made all the difference.

As for my destiny . . . well, let's just say it doesn't involve ribbons and hoops. I'm thinking more along the lines of first woman president, space explorer, Mrs. Matt Damon. . . . Whatever it is, I'll keep you posted.

PART
TWO

"**O**kay, listen up!" Coach Kelly bellowed. "Today we'll be participating in the Presidential Fitness Challenge!"

Why can't it be the Presidential Something-That-Lizzie's-*Good*-At Challenge?

Lizzie stifled a yawn as she turned to Miranda and Gordo on the gym-nauseum bleachers. It was almost lunchtime and the room was way warm. "I don't want a challenge," she whispered. "I want a nap."

"Guys, keep it down!" rasped Lizzie's long-time crush-boy Ethan Craft. "The president's gonna be here!"

Gordo suppressed a snicker and Lizzie and Miranda winced. With a sigh, Lizzie gazed at Ethan and lamented that sometimes a girl just has to accept that *major* hotness can come with *minor* brain power.

"The goal of this exercise is to hang on the bar until your arms fall off," Coach Kelly explained. She pointed to the tall pull-up bar in front of them. It was long enough to accommodate two boys and two girls.

Coach Kelly had combined the boys' and girls' PE classes a few times before—like when they'd learned square dancing together. Of course, the Presidential Fitness Challenge probably wouldn't involve do-si-dos or swinging your partner "till the cows came home."

On the bleachers, Gordo raised his hand.

The teacher nodded. "Mr. Gordon."

"What exactly does hanging on a bar have to do with fitness?" he asked.

The teacher puzzled over this for a second. "Take it up with the president," she finally barked, then she looked down at her clipboard roster. "All right! Sanchez, Gordon, Craft, McGuire! You're up!"

Oh, joy, thought Lizzie as she stood below the bar with Miranda, Gordo, and Ethan. They all reached up, took hold of the bar above them, and waited.

"Ready," called the teacher, setting her stopwatch. "One, two, three!"

The four of them quickly pulled themselves

up until their chins were over the bar. Lizzie thought it was totally easy.

Hanging from a bar isn't a real useful skill, but it's not exactly gym death.

"This isn't as bad as I thought it would be," Lizzie declared.

"Yeah," said Miranda, struggling to keep from slipping. "Piece . . . of . . . cake." Two seconds later, Miranda was gone. "Aaaaahhhh!" she cried as she dropped like a rock to the gym floor.

"Sanchez down!" bellowed the teacher and scribbled her time down on her clipboard.

"Y'know," said Gordo, beginning to sweat, "I bet the president doesn't have to do this. I couldn't imagine him having breakfast with heads of state and then going to his Oval

Office to do hanging chin-ups—" Gordo stopped talking when he realized he wasn't going to make it another second on the bar. "Aaaaaahhh!" he cried, then he was gone.

"Gordon down!" cried the coach.

Still effortlessly hanging on the bar, Lizzie stole a glimpse at Ethan. It was just the two of them now, she realized. How romantic! "So. Getting tired yet?" she asked her crush-boy.

Ethan swallowed. Beads of sweat had broken out on his forehead. "I'm just warming up," he claimed.

"Yeah," agreed Lizzie with a carefree grin. This'll be such a sweet A, she thought.

Coach Kelly checked her watch and nodded with approval. "Keep it up, McGuire and Craft," she coaxed. "Ten more seconds, you set a new school record."

Lizzie's eyes widened. "Did you hear that, Ethan?" she asked.

"Yeah. Record," Ethan managed to respond as his sweaty hands struggled to hang on. Two seconds later, he felt his grip giving way. "Hey, the bar. It's all slippery," he wailed. "No fair!"

But Lizzie was in her own little record-setting world. "That would be so cool," she pondered, still holding herself in the chin-up position. "Lizzie and Ethan breaking a school record," she went on. "Did you hear that, Ethan?"

Lizzie waited for Ethan to agree, but he didn't say a word. "Ethan?"

Finally, Lizzie turned her head. She was hanging on the bar *alone*.

Ethan has left the building!

"All right," Coach Kelly announced to the

class. "Let's have a hand for Ms. McGuire, new school record holder in the Presidential Fitness Challenge!"

On the bleachers, all the gym students started to clap for Lizzie. Amazed, she finally let go of the bar. Looks like I'm not just fit, thought Lizzie, I've got *presidential* fitness!

Time to pack my bags! Guess who's taking over the White House in 2024!

At lunch an hour later, Lizzie, Miranda, and Gordo were sitting at a table together on the sunny patio outside the cafeteria.

"I still don't think you need to hang on a bar to become president," Gordo grumbled. "I don't remember reading that in the Constitution."

Miranda rolled her eyes. Get over it, Gordo, she thought, then turned to Lizzie. "Well, I still can't believe you beat everyone. I mean, including Ethan!"

Lizzie shrugged. "It's not that big of a deal." She took a sip of juice and grinned. "Okay, it was really cool."

All in a day's work.

Just then, Ethan approached their lunch table with one of his jock friends. Thomas was a good-looking and popular student at Hillridge. In fact, Lizzie had to admit, he was a lot like Ethan—just a much sharper crayon in the jock box.

"Hey, Lizzie," called Thomas.

Lizzie smiled. "Hey, Thomas."

"I heard you wiped the floor up with my boy Ethan," he said, gesturing to his friend.

Ethan gave her a good-natured nod. "I just came over to give props to the new school record holder. Lizzie, I'd shake your hand, but I don't want you to *break* it." He smiled. Lizzie blushed.

"Don't worry, Ethan," she teased. "I'm not going to hurt you."

"Except for your *pride*," Miranda blurted out.

"Miranda!" Lizzie cried, seeing Ethan's smile turn into an embarrassed frown.

Lizzie was happy she'd broken the record in gym class, but she was *so* not willing to let it hurt her friendship with Ethan. Sometimes, thought Lizzie in frustration, Miranda just doesn't know when to keep her big, blunt mouth *shut*.

Thomas elbowed his friend. "Oh, Ethan, are you gonna take that?" he teased.

Ethan thought it over and shrugged. "I'm up for a rematch," he announced. "If the lady is."

Gordo shook his head. "Oh, that's a shocker. 'Ooooh. I lost to a girl. And now to reassert my male dominance, I need to beat her in front of all my friends.'"

"It's not like that, Gordon," Ethan replied firmly. Then he looked a little sheepish. "'Cause I don't know what that means."

"Don't worry, Ethan," Lizzie said quickly, trying to make things okay. "It was just this one little weird thing that happened today in gym class. That's all."

But Thomas wasn't letting it go that easily. "Hey, you guys could arm wrestle," he suggested loudly—so loudly that the kids sitting at the other lunch tables on the patio started to take notice.

Ethan scratched his chin, considering his chances. He figured they were better than good. "What do you say, McGuire?" he challenged.

"Yes!" cried Miranda.

Lizzie's brow furrowed. Arm wrestling a guy seemed pretty silly, but all these kids were looking at them expectantly. Plus, she thought, it's a chance to hold hands with Ethan Craft! "Sure," she agreed.

Lizzie rose from her chair, moved down the table, and sat down opposite Ethan. At the same time, boys and girls from nearby lunch tables moved to stand around them. If Ethan Craft was actually going to arm wrestle Lizzie McGuire, then nobody wanted to miss it!

Lizzie and Ethan put their elbows on the table surface and clasped hands.

"Okay," said Miranda, putting her own

hand on top of theirs. "I'm going to say 'one-two-three-go.' Start on 'go.' Got it?"

"Got it," said Ethan and Lizzie.

"One . . . two . . . three . . . *go*!" Miranda cried.

For a second, Lizzie and Ethan's hands didn't budge. Their arms seemed to be applying equal pressure to each other. Then, very slowly, Ethan began to take the lead, pushing Lizzie's arm down toward the table a few inches.

"Lizzie, Lizzie, Lizzie," said Ethan with a confident smile.

The boys in the crowd started to whoop and shout. Lizzie grit her teeth and dug in. She slowly began to push Ethan's arm back, bit by bit. The girls in the crowd began to cheer and clap.

Ethan fought back, moving Lizzie's arm the other way, but Lizzie totally focused and

Ethan's arm was soon sinking toward the table. A hush of disbelief fell over the crowd. Ethan was now inches away from *losing*!

"Lizzie! Lizzie! Lizzie!" Ethan finally said again, but this time he didn't sound confident. He sounded freaked out.

In a final burst of strength, Lizzie slammed Ethan's hand down all the way. Stunned, the crowd went completely silent.

"I won!" Lizzie cried. Whoa, she thought, looks like all that rhythmic gymnastics training really left me pumped.

Realizing they'd just witnessed something totally amazing, the kids around her went wild.

CHAPTER TWO

It was a universally acknowledged notion that Matt McGuire was an evil genius—except when it came to math.

". . . and you will not leave this room until you are done with your homework!" declared Mrs. McGuire, finishing her after-school lecture.

Matt sighed at the desk in his bedroom. For a week now, he'd been blowing off his teacher's assignments. Ms. Chapman had finally called today to tell Mrs. McGuire she'd had enough of Matt not doing his homework.

"Mom, have you ever thought that maybe I wasn't meant to do math?" asked Matt calmly.

"No," snapped Mrs. McGuire. Then she turned on her heel and firmly shut the door.

"This is so unfair," Matt griped.

He looked around for something, *anything,* to do but the stack of difficult multiplication problems on the desk in front of him.

Ahhhh, he thought, *computer games.* He turned on his PC. But his mother had already locked it. Her face popped up and began floating around the monitor chanting, "Do your homework! Do your homework! Do your homework!"

Matt shuddered and quickly turned off the terrifying screen saver. "She's good," he had to admit.

He looked around again. Come on, he

thought, there must be another possible time-waster around here. On the desk, he zeroed in on a roll of tape. He reached for it and began pulling off long strips.

Thirty minutes later, Mrs. McGuire opened Matt's bedroom door and walked in carrying a snack tray. Matt swung around in his desk chair and clawed the air with his fingers. "I am Tape-zilla! Fear me!" he screeched.

Mrs. McGuire stared at her son. He had wrapped enough tape around his face to make him look like The Mummy. She had only one thing to say to him: "Matt, do your home-work."

Mrs. McGuire set the tray on Matt's desk, then headed for the door. "And have fun getting that tape off your face, Tape-zilla," she called over her shoulder.

Matt's brow furrowed in confusion. What the heck does she mean by that? he wondered.

Five seconds later, Mrs. McGuire heard the sound of tape ripping inside Matt's bedroom, followed by Matt's "Aaaaaaaaaahhhhhhhhh!"

Mrs. McGuire just smiled.

At his bedroom desk, Matt put the raw skin of his face down on the cool wood surface. After a few minutes, he started to snooze.

A few minutes later, his window curtains rustled as a small, hairy visitor peeked through. Fredo, the chimp who lived down the block, scrambled over the windowsill and onto Matt's desk.

While Matt slept, Fredo noticed the math homework sitting there and picked up a pencil. He began to scribble on the paper, answering each multiplication problem one by one. When he was finished, the chimp drank down the glass of juice, then unpeeled the banana and ate it before climbing back out the window.

Just then, Matt abruptly woke up from his nap. "Vampires!" he cried with wide eyes. He shook his head, realizing he'd been dreaming. "Hey!" he cried in surprise when he glanced down at this homework paper. "Looks like this is done."

So, okay, he thought to himself, some people sleep*walk*. I guess I do sleep-*homework*. He patted himself on the back. "Good job, Matt."

Meanwhile, across town at the Digital Bean café, Lizzie, Miranda, and Gordo were hanging out, sipping smoothies. All sorts of people were coming over to their table and pointing Lizzie out as the girl who beat Ethan Craft at arm wrestling.

"Hey, Lizzie, make a muscle," called Thomas, striding up to their table with a big grin.

Lizzie flexed for him, then giggled. Ethan walked up behind Thomas. "Hey, what's up?" he said, then cut to the chase. "We need a fifth for flag football."

Gordo quickly shook his head. "Oh, sorry, Ethan, but I—"

"I was talking to Muscles McGuire over here," Ethan clarified.

"Yeah, c'mon, Lizzie," coaxed Thomas. "Are you game?"

Lizzie glanced from cute Thomas to even cuter Ethan.

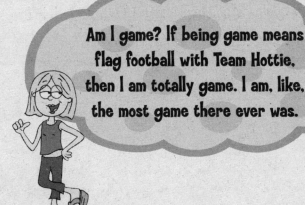

Am I game? If being game means flag football with Team Hottie, then I am totally game. I am, like, the most game there ever was.

"Sure, I'm game," she told them.

"Coolie," said Ethan. "See you tomorrow after school?"

"I'm there," she replied.

After Ethan and Thomas strode away, Miranda turned to her suddenly jock-friendly friend. "You are taking me with you," she demanded. "I don't care if I have to be a cheerleader, I'm going. If I had known *this* was gonna happen, I'd have *so* hung on the bar longer."

"Yeah, well, I guess I'll go, too," said Gordo. "But I am *not* gonna be a cheerleader."

"That's okay, Gordo," said Lizzie. "I don't think you have the legs for it, anyway."

CHAPTER THREE

The next day at school, Matt held his breath as his teacher began handing back the previous night's homework assignments.

"I must say," Ms. Chapman announced to her students, "I was most *un*impressed with your math homework."

The class groaned.

"However," she added, "I'd especially like to single out Matt McGuire."

Uh-oh, thought Matt, slumping down at

his desk. I guess my whole sleep-homework thing isn't going to work after all.

"As we all know, Matt isn't exactly a role model for class conduct," Ms. Chapman continued.

That was the understatement of the century, thought Matt's girlfriend, Melina Bianco, sitting at the desk next to him. She giggled and glanced at Matt, who slumped farther down in his seat.

"But," added the teacher, "he's a perfect example of how hard work and perseverance pays off!"

Melina's amused look changed to one of complete confusion. Stunned, she watched Ms. Chapman hand Matt back his homework. "A 97, Mr. McGuire," the teacher told him with a big smile. "Nice work."

As Ms. Chapman walked back to the front of the classroom, Melina turned to Matt. "I don't believe it," she whispered. "How?"

Matt shrugged. "I'm brilliant?"

Melina gave Matt an extremely skeptical look.

"Okay," he admitted quietly, "here's how it happened. I was in my room about to dig into *my* homework when I fell asleep. When I woke up, it was done."

"Fine," said Melina. "But tonight you're taking home my homework." She handed over her homework problems.

Matt smiled at Melina's bedazzling blue eyes and golden hair. "I'll sleep through the whole day, if I have to, to finish your homework," he promised.

Meanwhile, over at the junior high, classes ended for the day, and Lizzie changed into a tank top and sweats in the girls' lavatory, then headed for the athletic field. It felt good to be outside. The sun was shining brightly and the grass smelled clean and fresh.

Lizzie greeted Ethan, Thomas, and the other flag-football players who were just taking the field. Lizzie quickly fastened the belt around her waist that held the two long flags and jogged out to join Ethan's team.

A bunch of kids were watching from the bleachers at the side of the field. Among them, Miranda and Gordo waved. Lizzie nervously waved back.

For most of the game, Lizzie just hung in there, not sure what to do. Mostly, she just watched the action and tried to run along with the ball as the boys moved it up and down the grass.

Near the end of the game, Ethan's team had scored the most points. But the other team had time for one more play. If they scored a goal, Ethan's team would lose.

"All right," said Ethan, getting his four teammates into a huddle, "it's gonna be a pass! We gotta go man-to-man!"

They broke from the huddle and faced the offensive team. "Cover the flat," Ethan advised Lizzie. "We gotta hold 'em!"

Lizzie gulped. "Huh? What does that mean?"

All right, this is weird. Ethan's usually the one who's confused.

"'Cause, if we hold 'em," he explained very slowly and carefully, "we win. 'Cause the team with the most points wins. And we're that team!"

"No, I meant the flat part," clarified Lizzie just as the ball was snapped. Wait! she thought. Things are moving too fast! But the quarterback had already thrown the ball to this cutie named Jose, who caught the ball and started to run.

"Hey, who's covering Jose?" cried Ethan. "Thomas!"

But Thomas was too far away. In fact, everyone was. Lizzie instantly realized that she was the only player close enough to catch Jose. She immediately took off after the cutie, racing down the field like a wild woman.

Nobody scores on my watch!

Just a few yards from the goal line, Lizzie made a desperate leap toward Jose, reaching out for his flag but taking him down in the process. They landed together in a puddle of mud.

"Ow," Jose complained to Lizzie as he rose from the muck. "It's *flag* football. Not tackle."

Lizzie shrugged. "Sorry."

The rest of the players jogged over. Thomas rushed up to Lizzie. Her clothes, arms, and face were now spattered with mud, but she hardly noticed. "Was that okay?" she asked her teammate.

"Okay?" said Thomas. "Lizzie, look at you, you're a monster! You won us the game!"

"You got some righteous moves, McGuire," said Ethan. "Hey, we got another game tomorrow."

"Yeah, you *will* be there, right?" insisted Thomas.

"Sure," said Lizzie. "It was totally fun!"

"Props, Lizzie," said Ethan with a grin. "You're a total dude."

As Thomas and Ethan jogged off the field, Gordo and Miranda approached her. "Lizzie, that was a *great* hit," said Gordo. "You totally took Jose out!"

"Yeah," agreed Miranda, "and you're hanging with all the cute guys all over the place. I mean, who are you?"

"I'm a total dude," said Lizzie proudly.

Finally, the cute boys notice me.

"That's right, Lizzie," sneered a familiar voice. It was Kate Sanders, looking like she'd just stepped off a fashion runway—perfect hair, perfect clothes, perfect makeup, and teeth blindingly whitened. "You *are* a total dude," she told Lizzie. "You act like a dude, you look like a dude—" With a little exhale of revulsion, she pinched her upturned nose.

"You even *smell* like a dude." Then with a wave of her manicured hand, Kate turned to leave. "Later," she tossed over her shoulder, pointedly adding, "*dude.*"

Lizzie grimaced. Kate's nasty words were forcing her to rethink everything that had just happened.

Yeah, the cute boys notice me. Because they think I'm one of them.

That night in bed, Lizzie tossed and turned. Suddenly, she awoke to find Ethan, Thomas, and Kate standing over her. Ethan and Thomas didn't look happy with her anymore. In fact, they looked totally disgusted by her. "You're a total dude, Lizzie," Ethan said with a grimace of revulsion.

"You're a monster!" cried Thomas in horror.

"That's right, Lizzie. You *are* a total dude," said Kate, then she laughed like a crazed witch—which totally wasn't a stretch in Lizzie's opinion.

At that moment, Lizzie *really* awakened. "Aaaah!" she cried, bolting upright in bed. Frantically, she glanced around her room, but Kate, Ethan, and Thomas were gone. She glanced at the clock. 5:30 A.M.

I haven't been awake *this* early since I quit rhythmic gymnastics!

Way too disturbed to go back to sleep, Lizzie reached for the phone on the nightstand. She speed-dialed Miranda.

"Five more minutes, Mom," the groggy voice murmured on the other end of the line.

"Miranda, it's me, and I know that it's 5:30 in the morning and I'm really, really sorry, but I need you."

Miranda's eyes were still closed. Slowly, she opened them. "Lizzie, did I just call you in my sleep?" she asked seriously confused. "I just woke up and the phone was in my hand."

"Miranda, everybody thinks that I'm a guy," Lizzie explained desperately. "Ethan called me a total dude, and Thomas said I was a monster."

"Lizzie, maybe you're a guy-girl," offered Miranda.

"But that's just it, Miranda," replied Lizzie. "No guy is ever gonna wanna take me on a date, or to dances, or to the movies, or anything."

The guys will high-five me, but they won't hold my hand.

"Maybe I could be more of a girly-girl," Lizzie proposed.

Miranda yawned. "Good idea," she said, then sighed. "Lizzie, I love you and all, but next time could you please schedule a crisis for the *daylight* hours?"

"Sure," said Lizzie.

"Thank you."

Miranda hung up and Lizzie jumped out of bed with total determination.

Okay, they want a girl? I can be a total girl. I'm going to be the *girliest* girl they've ever seen!

CHAPTER FOUR

While Lizzie was rising and shining and changing her outfit a half dozen times, Matt remained in bed, sleeping. On his desk sat two bananas, two glasses of juice, and two sets of math homework—one for him and one for Melina.

Just as he had before, Fredo the chimp crawled in through the open window to steal Matt's snack. When he noticed the math problems sitting on Matt's desk, he automatically picked up a pencil and scribbled out all the answers. Then he drank the juice, ate the bananas, and scrambled back out the window.

Matt woke abruptly. "No more gravy!" he cried, then shook his head clear of his weird Thanksgiving Day dream and rose from bed. Sleepily, he crossed the room and checked out the homework problems he'd left on his desk.

"Looks like this is done," he murmured, scanning the newly scribbled answers. Matt patted himself on the back and thought, this sleep-homework thing is the bomb!

"Who's your math genius?! Who is your math genius?!" he cried, dancing around the room. At this rate, he thought, I'll be able to ace high school, college, and grad school with just a few sleeping pills. And after that, who knows what I can accomplish while completely unconscious?

"Why, thank you for that Nobel Prize!"

* * *

For the next couple of hours, Lizzie remained in total "girl" mode. She started with a spa treatment—mud mask, hot oil hair conditioning, and a manicure.

She applied her makeup with extra care and rifled her closet like a desperate diva.

Okay, I need one part *Clueless* and two parts *Legally Blonde.*

Outfit number one was too rock-star edgy, outfit number two was too tomboy casual, outfit number three was just plain dorky. *Nothing's right!* she wailed to herself.

"This is impossible," Lizzie said with a sigh.

She tried two more outfits, then finally put together the exact right one—a super feminine crocheted top in a pastel peachy color; a spotless pair of *un*faded designer low riders; and high-heeled sandals.

Watch out, world! . . . Miss Lizzie McGuire is ready to make your acquaintance.

At school that morning, Lizzie didn't just walk down the hallway, she *glided* with dainty little steps, swinging her small flowered handbag, which perfectly matched her crocheted top. I am a vision of girliness, she decided as she smiled demurely at her classmates.

When Ethan and Thomas spotted her, they crossed over to talk. "Hey, Ethan. Hi, Thomas," sang Lizzie in a sweet, breathless voice.

Ethan didn't seem to notice Lizzie's new

supergirlyness. In fact, when he eyed her high-heeled sandals, his brow furrowed with worry. "So, did you bring clothes to change into?" he asked.

Lizzie shook her head. "For what?"

"The game, Lizzie," said Thomas in frustration. "I mean, we gotta have our number-one tackler!"

Lizzie tried flipping her hair à la Kate. "Oh, I think I'm finished with football," she told them.

"What. Why?" said Thomas. "I thought you were having a blast yesterday."

"You tore up the field," agreed Ethan.

Tore up the field? I chewed it up and spit it out! I totally rocked and don't you forget it!

"Yeah, well," said Lizzie, "I just don't think football's my sport. But—" She did the Kate flip with her hair again. "I'll come by and cheer you guys on."

Ethan and Thomas felt a little betrayed as Lizzie glided away. "We don't need another cheerleader, we need a player," complained Thomas.

Ethan shook his head with disappointment. "I guess girls really don't play football."

Who you calling a girl? . . . Oh. That's me.

By lunchtime, Lizzie's predawn spa session had finally caught up with her. She was sitting with Miranda and Gordo at their usual patio table when Gordo started talking about some documentary he'd watched on TV the night before. Lizzie tried to concentrate, but her eyelids just kept getting heavier. The good news was that when her head finally hit the table, the fall was cushioned by her potato salad.

"Lizzie?" called Gordo, shaking her arm. "You're falling asleep in your food."

Lizzie didn't respond.

"Yeah," Miranda added, "it's not very *girly.*"

That did it. Lizzie pulled her head up. She now had potato salad in her hair. Miranda picked it out.

"Girly?" said Gordo, glancing from Lizzie to Miranda. "What are you guys talking about?"

"Well," Miranda began, "Ethan thinks of Lizzie as a guy-friend, so now all of his guy-friends think of her as a guy-friend so now she's Lizzie the guy-friend who real guys won't ever ask out."

"So, basically, I'm just a guy-girl," Lizzie finished.

Gordo blinked, still totally confused. "Okay."

"Let me explain it to you," Lizzie tried again. "I've been up since 5:30 this morning—"

"—and called me, thank you very much," Miranda noted.

"Let me finish," Lizzie insisted. "It took me twice as long to do my hair and makeup this morning, and I changed my outfit six times. That's three more than I usually do."

"Well, you don't really look any different, Lizzie," said Gordo. "At least, not to me."

Lizzie's face fell—but not in her potato salad. She was disappointed to hear that all her efforts were for naught. "See?" she wailed to Miranda. "It doesn't even make a difference. I'm doomed to be a guy-girl forever."

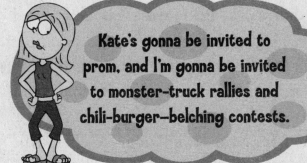

Kate's gonna be invited to prom, and I'm gonna be invited to monster-truck rallies and chili-burger—belching contests.

Exhausted and crushed, Lizzie put her head back down on the table.

"Ah, Lizzie," called Gordo, "you're getting potato salad in your hair again."

Miranda sadly shook her head. "Just let her rest."

Later that day, Matt came home from school to find his parents sitting on the living room couch watching TV. They immediately called him over.

"Hey, Matt, we got a call from your school today," Mr. McGuire informed him.

"I didn't do it! I was framed!" cried Matt.

Mrs. McGuire patted the spot on the couch next to her. "Sit down," she told him.

Matt sat.

"We got a call from your teacher, Ms. Chapman," Mrs. McGuire clarified.

"Yeah. She said your math has really improved," added Mr. McGuire. "Two A's in a row."

Mrs. McGuire smiled with motherly pride. "Now, I know we've been very hard on you about the homework," she said. "But obviously, it's working, so we just wanted to tell you that we are very, very proud of you."

"Wait," said Matt. "You're proud of *me*?"

"So what was it, buddy?" asked Mr. McGuire curiously. "What made the difference?"

"I, uh . . ." Matt began, then hesitated. What if my parents think this whole sleep-homework thing is just too weird, he wondered. What if they notify the authorities? Where will it lead? Laboratory experiments . . . psychiatric tests . . . sleep deprivation studies . . . brain surgery? Matt shuddered.

"I just buckled down," he lied. "Because when the going gets tough, Matt McGuire gets going!" He even punched the air with his fist to make his answer look good.

"All right," said Mr. McGuire, high-fiving his son.

Yeah, right, Matt told himself. You'd better get going before they ask you more questions. "Like now!"

As Matt raced out of the family room, Mr.

and Mrs. McGuire gazed after him, their eyes filled with disgustingly gushy parental pride.

"See ya," Mr. McGuire called to his brilliant son. Then he turned to his wife. "You know, I knew he'd come around. He takes after *me*, y'know."

Mrs. McGuire raised a skeptical eyebrow. As far as she knew, her husband was *terrible* at math. But in the interest of family harmony, she decided to let it go.

CHAPTER FIVE

Near the end of the school day, Lizzie decided to talk to the one person who'd started her down this whole guy-girl path: Coach Kelly. She found the teacher working out with a medicine ball in the gymnasium.

"Hey, McGuire! Catch!" the teacher called as she good-naturedly tossed the medicine ball. But Lizzie was so distracted by her problems, she didn't even attempt to catch it. It fell with a thud to the gym floor.

"What?" teased the coach. "You can hang all day, but you can't catch a medicine ball?"

Lizzie picked up the ball and handed it to her muscle-bound teacher. "Sorry," she said.

Coach Kelly walked over to her. "I heard you beat Craft in arm wrestling yesterday. Nice job."

Yeah, nice job of permanently ruining any chance I may have of a social life.

"Thanks," Lizzie replied flatly.

"You don't sound too happy about the whole thing," observed the coach.

"Well, I'm not," Lizzie admitted. "Ever since gym class yesterday, everybody thinks that I'm a guy-girl. I'm never gonna get a date."

"They think you're a guy-girl because

you set a school record?" asked the teacher.

"*And* I beat Ethan Craft in arm wrestling," added Lizzie, "*and* I played flag football."

"Who exactly thinks this?" asked the coach, walking over to a stack of mats to grab a quick drink from her water bottle.

"Everyone!" cried Lizzie, throwing up her hands. "Ethan Craft said I was a 'total dude.' And Thomas called me a 'monster.'"

Coach Kelly started to laugh. When Lizzie appeared confused, she sat down on the mats and explained, "Craft calls everyone a dude. He doesn't know many other words. And Thomas is a guy. To him, *monster* is a compliment."

"But Kate thinks it, too," wailed Lizzie.

"Did you ever think that maybe Kate's jealous of the fact that you're spending quality time with the really cute boys in class?" asked the coach.

Lizzie blinked. "No."

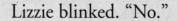

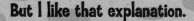
But I like that explanation.

"There are people that think being strong is a boy thing," Coach Kelly admitted, "but that's because they're severely lacking in brains."

Lizzie sighed. "I guess." But it still didn't solve her problem.

"Hear me out, McGuire. Do you think that Brandi Chastain worries about what people think? Or what about Picabo Street or Kelly Clark?"

Lizzie shook her head and replied, "I'm not like them." Which was a total understatement as far as Lizzie was concerned. Brandi Chastain was a U.S. Women's Soccer gold medal winner. Picabo Street was a two-time medalist in Olympic skiing, and Kelly Clark was a snowboarding superstar. "They're champions," Lizzie protested.

"Just because you like to play flag football, it doesn't mean you can't do more girly things, too," Coach Kelly replied. "I mean, I'm a power lifter—" To make her point, the teacher raised her beefy arms and flexed her huge biceps. "But I still like to go swing dancing with Mr. Lang."

Lizzie's eyes widened. "You like to swing dance? I can't believe it."

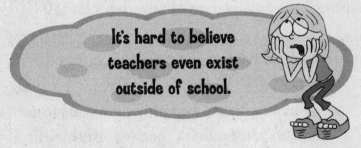

It's hard to believe teachers even exist outside of school.

"Well, believe it," insisted the coach. "I

even sew my own dresses 'cause I can't find any to fit my arms."

"That's really cool," said Lizzie. "So you can do both."

"And so can you, McGuire."

Lizzie nodded. "Thanks. I feel a lot better now."

"No problem. I *can* talk to students," said the teacher with a little smile. "I just prefer to yell most of the time."

Lizzie returned the coach's smile, then thanked her one more time and headed off to the girls' lavatory. Now that she'd changed her mind—it was time to change her clothes!

Meanwhile, back at the McGuire house, Matt was hard at work on his homework—which meant he was fast asleep at his desk. As usual, a glass of juice and a banana were sitting on a tray. But this time when Fredo climbed through Matt's bedroom window, the chimp stopped and scratched his head. The math homework problems on Matt's desk didn't look the same as the ones he'd solved before.

Frustrated, Fredo poked Matt. With wide eyes, Matt woke up to find a chimp on his desk. "Fredo!" he cried. Fredo smiled and pointed at the math homework, and then the chimp shrugged.

Well, what do you know, thought Matt, the chimp's been doing my homework all along. That's *almost* as good as doing it in my sleep. But clearly there's some sort of issue here.

"What?" Matt asked Fredo. "You mean you haven't covered long division in monkey school yet?"

Fredo shook his head "no," then started to throw a fit, screaming and jumping around the bedroom, throwing up his long, hairy arms. Matt frantically tried to calm the chimp down. "Hey, it's okay! Really."

Suddenly, a loud knock sounded on Matt's bedroom door. Uh-oh, he thought. The door opened and in walked Matt's parents and his dad's two softball buddies, David and Jeremy—the ones who owned Fredo.

Matt gulped. "Hi," he said, trying to sound totally innocent.

"Fredo, you know you can't go out until you finish your homework," scolded David.

"Is he stuck on long division?" asked Matt without thinking. "Because he had no problem with yesterday's homework."

Together, Mr. and Mrs. McGuire gasped, and Matt instantly realized he should have kept his big mouth shut. "Oopsie," he murmured.

"Fredo, we've been over long division a thousand times, already," scolded Jeremy.

David turned to Jeremy. "You know, he wouldn't keep coming over here if we got him that satellite dish."

"Come on, Fredo," said Jeremy, taking the chimp's hairy little hand. David took the other and the two men left with their brainy chimp.

Immediately, Mr. McGuire turned to his not-so-brainy son. "So, you mean to tell us that that *monkey* got a 97 on your math homework?"

Matt winced. "Yeah."

Matt's mother looked steamed enough to blast off for Mars. "Matt, I am so furious with you," she snapped, looking to her husband to join her in the scolding.

But Mr. McGuire suddenly seemed lost in thought. "Hmmm . . ." he pondered aloud, "maybe Fredo can help us with our taxes."

Mrs. McGuire could not believe her

clueless husband. Great, she thought. My son has just been shown up by a primate and his father's response is to hire the chimp as an accountant!

"What?" asked Mr. McGuire, finally noticing his wife's glare.

"You're right," Mrs. McGuire told her math-challenged husband. "Matt *does* take after you."

Meanwhile, over on the Hillridge athletic field, Miranda and Gordo were walking Lizzie out to the flag football game.

"Are you sure you want to do this?" Miranda worriedly asked Lizzie.

"I'm positive," said Lizzie.

Let's play some football!

"I'm proud of you, Lizzie," said Gordo with a smile. "Go out there and kick some butt."

Just then, Kate stepped forward to snidely inspect Lizzie's sweats. "Who let the dogs out?" she quipped.

Lizzie stared at the girl. "Nobody likes you, Kate," she said flatly, then left the shocked, sputtering cheer queen in the dust as she approached Ethan. He was just coming off the field for a drink.

"I want in," Lizzie demanded.

"Sorry, McG," he told her. "Wouldn't want you to break a nail or anything."

"Ethan, I don't care if I break all of my nails. I'm going in."

Thomas overheard Lizzie as he jogged to the sidelines. "Look, Ethan, they're killing us out there." He turned to the former monster player who'd won them the game the day before. "Lizzie, we could really use you."

Lizzie looked expectantly at Ethan. "What do you say?"

"Lizzie," he replied, "if I put you in, then someone else will have to sit out."

Thomas stared at Ethan. "C'mon, Craft."

Ethan thought it over a second. "I got an idea."

That's something you don't hear very often.

Two minutes later, Lizzie made a great tackle in the muddy field—and Ethan was watching the game from the bench. He'd sidelined himself so Lizzie could play.

"Ethan!" cried Kate, frustrated that he wasn't listening to her.

"Dude, I told you, I'm watching the game!" he snapped.

Kate's eyes widened in horror. "I am *not* a *dude*!"

"Shhhhhhhhhh. Shh!" Ethan replied.

On the field, the quarterback cried, "Hike!" Then the halfback snapped the ball. Lizzie intercepted a pass and made a great running play, fighting off blockers to gain yard after yard until she scored a touchdown!

Gordo and Miranda went crazy. Then Miranda turned to Gordo. "They're gonna think of her as a guy-girl," she lamented.

"You know what?" said Gordo. "I don't think she cares what they think. And I think that's pretty cool."

Miranda smiled. "Yeah."

On the field, Thomas ran over and high-fived the muddy monster that was Lizzie McGuire. "Great play, Lizzie!" he told her. "I'm glad you showed up."

Lizzie nodded. "I know. Me too."

The sun was warm, the grass smelled sweet, and Lizzie was feeling better than good—because she was *finally* doing what she loved.

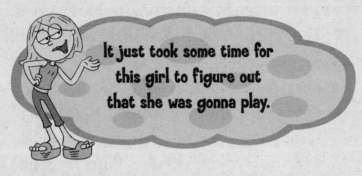

It just took some time for this girl to figure out that she was gonna play.

"So let's go out there and make those guys wish they were never born!" Lizzie exclaimed.

Thomas knew he couldn't have said it better. "All right!" he cried.